Three by the Sea

MINI GREY

On a pebbly stretch of shore
in a beach hut by the sea
there lived a black cat,
a white dog
and a little
grey mouse.

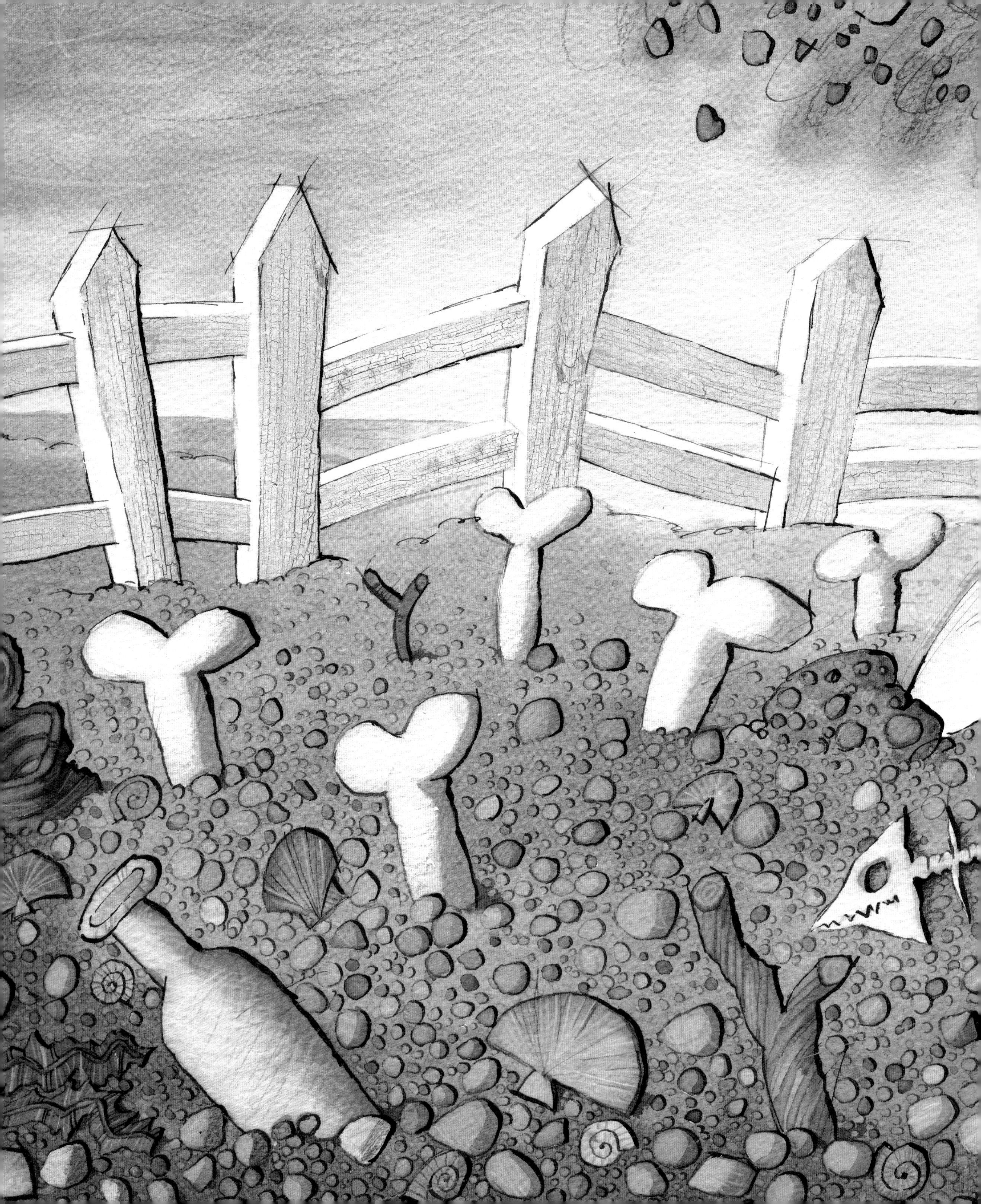

The dog tended
to the garden.

The cat took care of the housework.

The mouse
looked after
the cooking.

And they lived happily.

Or so they thought.

1001 FAVOURITE FONDUES
HOT CHEESE FONDUE
You will need:
Gruyère Cheese
Emmenthal Cheese
Cheddar Cheese
and for decoration:
Parmesan Cheese
METHOD
Grate the cheeses into a large cooking pot. Simmer on a gentle heat, stirring constantly until the cheeses are melted. On no account allow it to burn.
Decorate with shavings of Parmesan.
1001 FAVOURITE FONDUES
EXTRA CHEESY FONDUE
INGREDIENTS:
Roquefort Cheese
Gorgonzola Cheese
Stilton Cheese
Camembert Cheese
WHAT TO DO:
Keep the cheeses warm for several days until aromatic. Chop the cheeses finely and mix. Warm through in your fondue pot. Under no circumstances let your mixture boil quickly, otherwise it becomes tough and rubbery.
MOUSE & GARDEN
THE GOLLOPING GOURMET
WORLD GUIDE
GOOD MOUSEKEEPING'S COOKERY COMPENDIUM
WAVERLEY
ALL-PURPOSE FLAKES
ALL-PURPOSE FLAKES
Perfect for:
breakfast
snacks
baking
bathing
washing
rinsing
scouring
AND MANY MORE USES
INGREDIENTS
SUPERSTRONG GINGER BEER

One night
a Stranger blew in
to the shore

and found his way to
the beach hut by the sea.

He invited himself in.

The Stranger announced that they were the Lucky Winners of a visit from the ***WINDS OF CHANGE TRADING COMPANY*** and it would be absolutely FREE.

He explained that if you felt strangely discontented, or wondered if your life was missing a special Something, then ***WINDS OF CHANGE*** was the company for you.

And, of course, everything was ABSOLUTELY FREE.

The Stranger also explained
that he needed to sleep
in a proper bed
with plenty of pillows
and eiderdowns.

There was only one bed.

The next day, after breakfast,
the Stranger took Mouse aside and said
"You know, Mouse, I don't mean to be
rude about Dog, but his idea of
gardening is a bit odd.

He only plants bones!
Who wants a bone-garden?
Where are the flowers?
Where are the vegetables?
Where are the herbs?"

The Stranger
gave Mouse
some things to read
from his suitcase.

After lunch the Stranger
said to Dog:
"Dog – while you've been busy
digging the garden,
Cat has been doing the housework.
Come and look at Cat
doing the housework."

"Hmmm," said Dog.
"Well, we didn't sleep very well
last night."

But he felt a little upset.

The Stranger
gave Dog
a present too.

Around suppertime the Stranger found Cat alone and said:

"You know, Cat, I've never been that keen on fondue myself – but I suppose that mice never get tired of cheese. Do you have fondue every night?"

"Pretty much," said Cat.

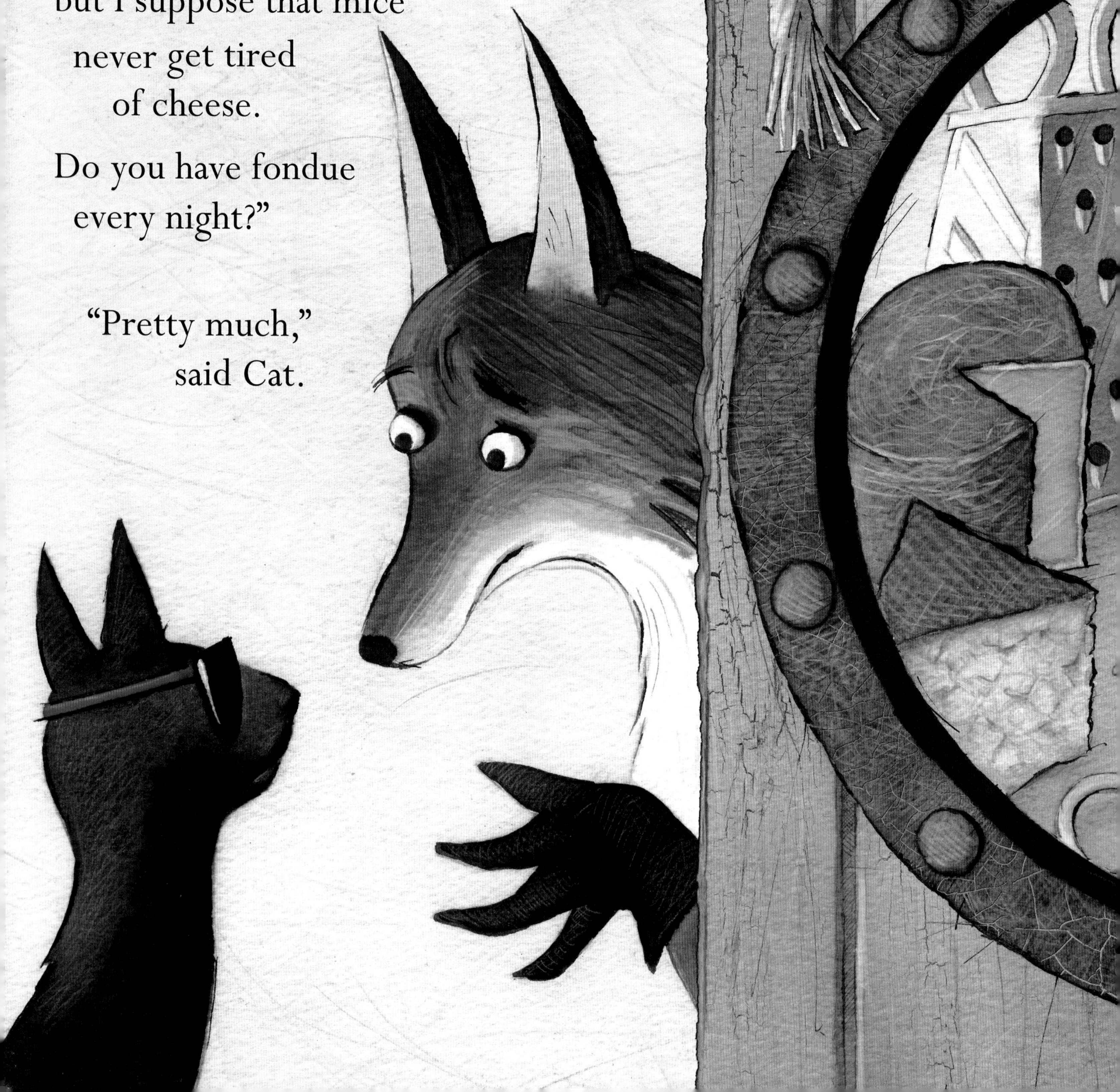

1001 FAVOURITE FONDUES

SUPER-WHIFFY
STILTON SURPRISE
An astonishingly pungent fondue
for the connoisseur

U WILL NEED:
rge lump of Stilton Cheese
Ripe Munster Cheese
kle of ancient Amorgos Cheese
Camembert and Gorgonzola to taste

METHOD:
arm the Stilton Lump through until
bubbling. Stir in th er cheeses
y gently until you n is filled
ful cheesy whiff
ith parsley and
ns.

APPETIT!

CAT BRAND
SARDINES

Cat also got
some gifts
from the suitcase.

WINDS OF CHANGE
MACKEREL IN TOMATO
SAUCE
A Feast of
Fresh Fish

At dinner
everyone was very quiet, until –
"A spot more fondue, anyone?"
asked Mouse,
and . . .

Why do we always have to have fondue?
Well you do the cooking then if you don't like it.
Maybe I will.
Well maybe you won't fall asleep while you're doing it.
What do you mean?
I saw you doing your so-called cleaning.
That's not fair Dog.
What about the garden?
When did we say that we
wanted a bone-garden?
Your cooking is horrible.
Your housework is rubbish.
Your garden's
a mess.

That night while Cat and Dog
were trying to sleep

Mouse was
packing his things,
planning to travel
to somewhere
where his cooking
was appreciated.

At about midnight the cat woke
with a lurch and a sinking feeling
that something was wrong.

She walked
along the sea front.
On the pebbles was a bundle
of things – the sort of things
that belonged to Mouse.

Through
the roar
of the sea
her keen ears
heard a desperate
far-away squeak.

Cat couldn't swim,
but she waded
into the water anyway.

She just had to
rescue Mouse.

Cat scooped up Mouse
and put him on her head,
but she was having trouble
staying afloat.

Then from
the watery darkness
a pale blob got
nearer and nearer
and nearer.

Dog was a good swimmer, good enough for all three of them.

Dog carried them all to safety by the shore.

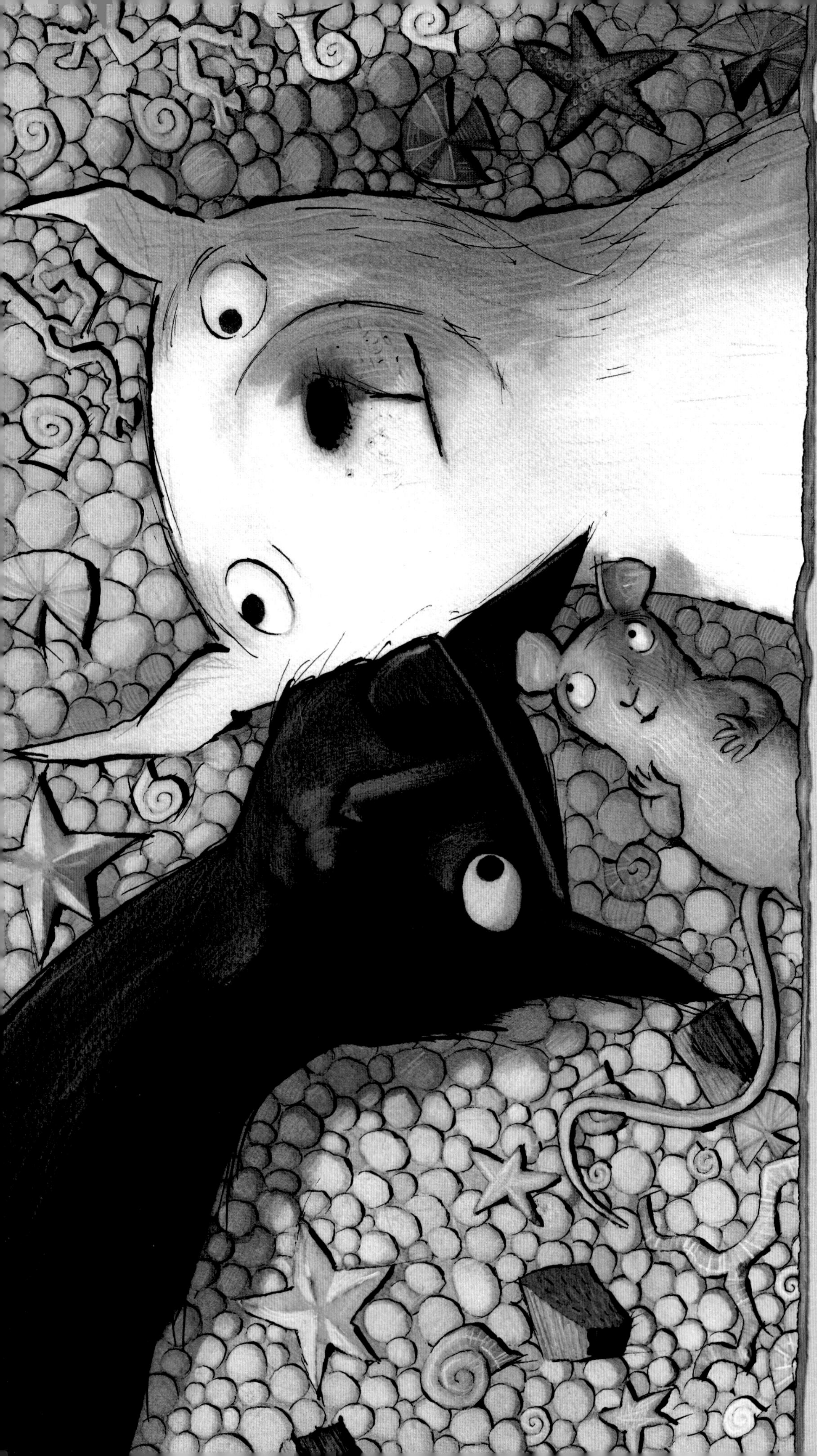

Back on the
beach
they made sure
that everyone
was still alive
and nobody
was drowned.

They all agreed
it was probably
time for
the Stranger
to leave.

But in the beach hut
there was not a shred
of the Stranger
or his suitcase.

Except a note,

and these packets
of seeds.

WINDS OF CHANGE
TRADING COMPANY LTD..

Called away on
Urgent Business.

Borrowed boat -
hope you don't mind.

Here is a last
FREE GIFT for you
from the
WINDS OF CHANGE
company.

Yours
A. Stranger Esq.

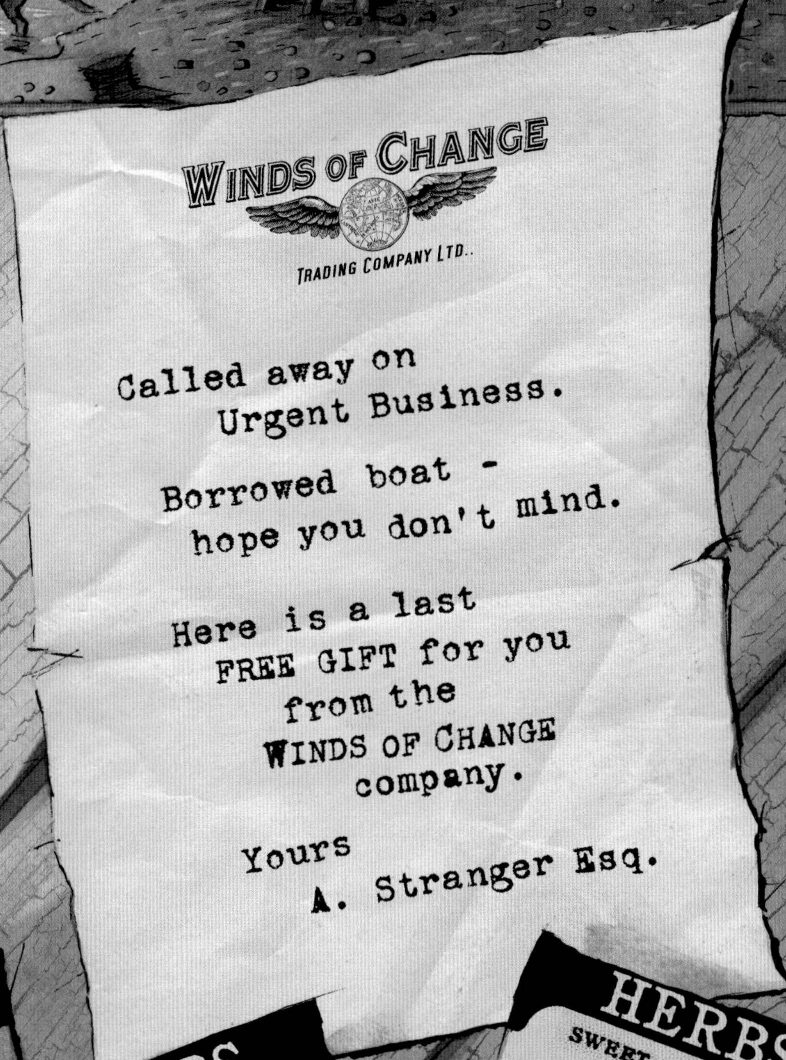

And now, if you happened to drop by
the beach hut near the sea
you might notice that they
are doing things
a little differently.

You might see
Mouse and Dog
cultivating their
Bone and Herb Garden.

Or you might see
Cat and Mouse making
Cheese and Pilchard Fondue
(with a twist of thyme and a bayleaf).

If it was first thing
in the morning
you'd most probably hear
Cat and Dog humming a tune
as they kept the hut
cosy and clean.

And you might
just notice
a scent of herbs
in the sea air.

FOR OUR OWN HERB

THREE BY THE SEA
A RED FOX BOOK 978 1 862 30809 1

First published in Great Britain by Jonathan Cape,
an imprint of Random House Children's Publishers UK
A Random House Group Company

Jonathan Cape edition published 2010
Red Fox edition published 2011

3 5 7 9 10 8 6 4 2

Red Fox Books are published by Random House Children's Publishers UK,
61–63 Uxbridge Road, London W5 5SA

www.randomhousechildrens.co.uk

Addresses for companies within The Random House Group Limited can be found at:
www.randomhouse.co.uk/offices.htm

THE RANDOM HOUSE GROUP Limited Reg. No. 954009

A CIP catalogue record for this book is available from the British Library.

Printed in China

SPECIAL THANKS TO THE BRAINPOWER OF ANDREA